Cover design by Véronique Lefève Sweet.

Little, Brown and Company
Hachette Book Group
1290 Avenue of the Americas, New York, NY 10104
Visit us at lb-kids.com

First Edition: March 2017

LB kids is an imprint of Little, Brown and Company. The LB kids name and logo
are trademarks of Hachette Book Group, Inc.

The publisher is not responsible for websites (or their content)
that are not owned by the publisher.

Library of Congress Control Number 2016949446

ISBNs: 978-0-316-50489-8 (hardcover), 978-0-316-50493-5 (ebook)

Printed in China

APS

10  9  8  7  6  5  4  3  2  1

The illustrations for this book were created digitally. This book was edited by Rex Ogle
and designed by Véronique Lefève Sweet. The production was supervised by
Rebecca Westall, and the production editor was Lindsay Walter-Greaney.
The text and display type were set in Ad Lib BT and Bubbleboddy Neue.

# Masha and the Bear®
## Kidding Around!

Adapted by **Lauren Forte**

Based on the episode "**Kidding Around**"

written by **Oleg Kuzovkov**

LITTLE, BROWN & COMPANY

**LB kids**

It is a beautiful sunny morning in the forest. The Bear cannot wait to go outside to fly his remote-controlled plane. He stands in his doorway, watching it soar through the sky.

Everyone else is also outside to enjoy the day. Sly Wolf and Silly Wolf, who are always hungry, are trying to catch butterflies to eat for lunch. But they are not having any luck.

Hare is collecting carrots so he can
eat, too. The ones that grow in the Bear's
garden are his favorites. He sneaks some
while the Bear isn't watching.

Pig decides to relax and take a swim. She swims back and forth through the puddle. It's very refreshing.

When Pig climbs out of the water, Masha
is waiting for her. "How is my baby feeling?"
Masha asks. "Tired after a swim?"
Pig shakes her head. But then, she sneezes.

"Are you sure that you didn't catch cold, my love?" Masha says. She puts Pig in a stroller. Masha loves to take care of her friends. "Don't you worry, my pretty. Mommy will get you well right away!"

Masha pushes Pig all the way up the hill to the old ambulance. There, she takes out all of the doctor's tools.

She even finds a doctor's outfit.
"Okay," Masha says. She gets ready
to examine Pig.

But Masha *accidentally* bumps the broken-down ambulance. It starts to roll down the hill!

*"Oops!"* Masha cries. The ambulance races down the hill, picking up speed. Masha grabs Pig's stroller and hurries after it.

The ambulance zooms down the road.
When Sly Wolf and Silly Wolf see it coming,
they run the other way!

Even Hare and his carrots are almost run over! It's a good thing he is so fast!

The stroller starts going faster than Masha can run. Soon she is trying to catch the ambulance *and* the stroller!

The Bear is startled as Sly, Silly, Hare—and even the butterflies—rush past him and into his house. The ambulance finally stops when it slams into the fence.

Pig's stroller stops, too, but she flies into the air! Luckily, she lands in the Bear's arms. Unluckily, the Bear's remote-controlled plane crashes and breaks.

Masha comes running up. "Everyone's okay? No one needs to see a doctor?" she asks. No one got hurt, but no one thinks everything is okay.

The Bear is very upset with Masha and gives her a time-out in the corner. "But I only wanted to play doctor," she says sadly.

The Bear remembers some of the trouble he got into when he was a little cub. One time he climbed a tree and ate a bunch of apples. He fell from the tree and rolled down the hill, bouncing along with all the fruit.

When he reached his yard, he *accidentally* knocked over all the beehives. He hadn't done it on purpose, but he still got in trouble.

His thoughts are interrupted by the sound of Pig and the others complaining.

But the Bear shushes them and asks whether *they* ever did something *by accident* when they were young.

Pig thinks back. She got dirty all the time, and it drove her mama crazy. Once, she even knocked her mama into a muddy puddle. *Accidentally, of course!*

Pig hadn't meant for it to end up that way. But she got a big time-out for it, too.

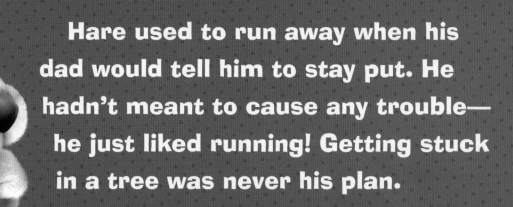

Hare used to run away when his dad would tell him to stay put. He hadn't meant to cause any trouble— he just liked running! Getting stuck in a tree was never his plan.

Squirrel had to rescue him. Hare's dad was so relieved that he was okay. But he still got put in time-out.

Silly and Sly do not want to share any of the trouble they used to get into. It must have been a lot!

But they all realize that Masha didn't mean to scare anyone. Sometimes, things happen *by accident*, not on purpose. So the friends go outside to help push the ambulance out of the yard.

The Bear finishes fixing his plane. He knows Masha feels bad. She is very sorry. So he calls over to her and holds up the plane.

The Bear lets Masha hold the remote and fly the plane. She loves it!

"Go higher and higher and higher! Like birds, you will fly in the sky!" she sings as she plays...

...before crashing the plane through the Bear's window. The Bear looks unhappy...

...but then he smiles and pulls Masha onto his lap. Maybe it's better if they fly the plane *together.*